Protocol and Other Stories

Femdom Mind Control

Flash Fiction – Vol. 42

S.B.

Disclaimer

This is a work of fiction. Names, characters, business, events, and incidents are the products of the author's imagination. Any resemblance to actual persons, living or dead, or actual events is purely coincidental. All characters are over 18.

Table of Contents

◎ An Accident - 1
◎ Being Good - 4
◎ Checking In - 7
◎ Defective - 13
◎ Doomed - 17
◎ Guest of Honor - 20
◎ Monthly Torment - 24
◎ Protocol - 27
◎ Running on Fumes - 30
◎ They're Coming - 33
◎ Time for Pain - 36
◎ You Want to Be Hypnotized - 39

Get ready to be activated.

My sincerest thanks to all patrons of Spell... B-O-U-N-D.

An Accident

Hi... you're awake! That's good, but please don't move and try not to speak more than you have to. There was a terrible accident and things are looking rather hectic. You're lucky someone brought you here immediately. Do you remember your name?

You do? Wonderful. Let me put it on my chart... Just one more question before the doctors take over from here. Can you tell me the name of a next of kin, friend, or girlfriend to contact to let them know what happened and that you're now in our care?

Oh? There's no one? Are you sure? Okay, being alone sucks, it's true, but I promise we'll do everything we can to help you deal with this. You've lost a lot of blood, but it will be okay. You're going to the ER right away and when you're done, I'll come to check on you again. See you soon.

(...)

"Madam President, It's Erin. I'm calling to inform you I believe we've found the perfect replacement. Yes, Madam President, I'm looking at the vital signs right now and the patient is stable. No relatives, no nothing, a life so bland that's easily forgettable... if we go through with the operation immediately, it's unlikely we'll ever face any repercussions. Yes, Madam President, I understand that unlikely doesn't mean it's 100% certain, but this is the best opportunity we've had in a long time. Are you really willing to lose millions waiting for approval that may never come? I urge you to do the right thing while you can, Madam President, otherwise you'll be facing the same problems as your predecessor in no time. No, Madam President, of course, this is not a threat. I'm merely speaking from experience with the Board. They'll want someone to blame if we don't give them the results they're after and you're always going to be the first in line. It's not a threat, but a statement of how things work in our line of business. Yes, Madam President, I'm convinced this is the way to go, so if I could have your approval... Fantastic! My team is ready, and we'll make you proud, trust me."

(...)

"Hello again. You've been unconscious for pretty much all day, but I'm happy to report that everything went smoothly. The procedure was a success, and you should be feeling the results soon. What? You're saying you heard me have a strange conversation on the phone about you? You're clearly confused, dear. It must result from the heavy sedation, but you'll be thinking clearly soon. No, we didn't rip open your chest to implant an alien creature inside, that's absurd! I think you need to sleep for a while longer to clear your mind. Let me adjust this and..."

(...)

"Madam President? It's Erin again. The transplant was a success, and the parasite is growing inside the patient now. As detailed in the files of Project Andromeda, once it reaches full maturation, it will take over the subject's mind, effectively wiping out any chance of resistance and, as you already know, the programming possibilities are endless, including.... Yes, Madam President, I'm sure we can arrange an 'accident' for any members of the Board that go against you. I'll get on it right away."

Being Good

Greta leaned against a lonely stone pillar, away from prying eyes, and sipping what appeared to be a glass of red wine, but Jonathan knew better. His older sister had been a person of peculiar tastes even from a tender age, but things had become increasingly chaotic following the conversion. She wasn't to blame for the event itself, but the same couldn't be said about the madness that followed. Restraint was something she hadn't mastered yet, and it was always on to him to clean up after her mess.

The party at Jonathan's house that night was almost dead, with the guests slowly drifting away, ready to return to their homes. Jonathan approached Greta, a spark of fury visible in his twinkling eyes, and said,

"We need to talk."

"Do we really?" she waved her right hand dismissively as if swatting an annoying fly.

"Yes. Damn it, Greta! You promised you would keep things under control tonight."

"And I did. I've been good, better than I expected to be if I may say so myself. Your friends and neighbors are still breathing, aren't they?"

"Not all of them," Jonathan reached for the inner pocket of his jacket, revealing the tip of a blood-soaked rag. "I just came from the study and found Laetitia lying there like a discarded rag doll. You made quite a mess, didn't you?"

"I suppose so... Don't worry, I'll clean everything once everyone else is gone," she replied, licking the underside of a protuberant sharp fang.

"That's not the point! Weren't you done killing people? And of all the ones you could have feasted on tonight, did you really have to go for her?"

"She caught me feeding, dear brother, and as much as I've grown used to pig's blood by now, it doesn't compare to the real deal."

"You're a bitch, Greta! Fuck!"

"Vampire bitch if you don't mind. And yeah, guilty as charged. Why are you freaking out though? Last time I checked, You didn't even like her!"

"Last time you checked..." he repeated, uncontrollably biting the nails on his right hand. "... but a lot of things changed in the last six months. Laetitia and I..."

"You what?"

"We were..."

"Oh, you were fucking? Okay, I had no idea you were that desperate for pussy! Come on, Jonathan, with plenty of fish in the sea, you really had to go for that one?"

"And what do you know, huh?" he growled. "You never cared for anyone even before you were bitten and got turned into this abomination! You can't possibly understand what we had and now you ruined everything!"

"No, I didn't. You know she'll be back. If your relationship was as real as you're implying, I'm sure it can survive a bite or two."

"You better be, because she's behind you right now," Greta smirked.

Jonathan turned on his heels to face the newly awakened fledgling with her silky black hair, icy eyes, and fresh puncture marks on her neck and wrists.

"Hi," she cooed. "It's so good to see you, my love."

"It is?" he gulped as the undead creature slid her wet tongue across his right cheek.

"Yes. You wouldn't believe the nightmare I just had."

"What did you dream about?"

"That I was starving all the time and that no one came to help me, but then I remembered you would never let me down, right?"

"I..." he muttered, staring into her dead and utterly irresistible eyes. "Greta, a little help here?"

"I think you should listen to her, dear brother. Listen and obey..."

"W-what? What happened to you being good?"

"Oh, I can be good, but that doesn't mean she has to be... Relax, brother. You'll love what comes next."

She was right. Sinking into his new owner's mesmerizing gaze, he returned to the dwindling festivities just in time to lock all the doors. The real party was only getting started.

Checking In

From: Allison <allywins2@hotmail.com>

Sent: 29 May 2022 17:30

To: Camille B. <notyouraveragegirl@protonmail.com>

Subject: What happened to you?

Hey, girl.

It's been a while. What's going on? You promised you'd be in touch after you settled in your new place, but it's been over a month. Why haven't you answered any of my calls or texts? I want to hear from you, so I hope you'll be so kind as to respond to this e-mail once you read it.

Kisses,

Allison

From: Camille B. <notyouraveragegirl@protonmail.com>

Sent: 30 May 2022 00:21

To: Allison <allywins2@hotmail.com>

Subject: Re: What happened to you?

Ally, hi.

I'm so sorry, you're right. I did promise that, but a lot of things happened since I left the country and I could never find the time to talk to you properly, so it slipped my mind. Please, don't think badly of me. The move went without a hitch and I'm really loving my new life out here. Right on the first day, I met an amazing person who completely changed my way of looking at things. I can't wait to tell you all about her, but it will have to wait until next time because I'm on my way out. Talk to you soon,

Cam

From: Allison <allywins2@hotmail.com>

Sent: 30 May 2022 02:22

To: Camille B. <notyouraveragegirl@protonmail.com>

Subject: Re: What happened to you?

I'm glad you're doing well, but I won't deny feeling peeved about you forgetting about me so easily. I'm curious about this amazing new person, though. What do you mean by completely changing the way you look at things? Are you saying you started playing for the other team?

Allison

From: Camille B. <notyouraveragegirl@protonmail.com>

Sent: 30 May 2022 15:59

To: Allison <allywins2@hotmail.com>

Subject: Re: What happened to you?

Me playing for the other team? No! I didn't become a lesbian overnight, Cam, and I can't believe that's what crossed your mind when I wrote what I did. Her name is Samantha, and she's a hypnotist, okay? She used to work as a hypnodomme, dominating men and women around the world for money, but has since slowed down to embrace a more pedestrian life. She still plays with people's minds occasionally and the things she already did to mine... She's truly something else and I wish you two could meet. I'm sure you'd love her as much as I do. You need to let me know when you're able to visit, okay?

Cam

From: Allison <allywins2@hotmail.com>

Sent: 30 May 2022 18:13

To: Camille B. <notyouraveragegirl@protonmail.com>

Subject: Re: What happened to you?

A hypnotist? That's unexpected, as you never seemed the sort of person who was interested in things like that. Frankly, I'm scared of letting anyone get inside my head, so even if I do get to meet this Samantha eventually, I think I'll pass on the offer. Tell me more of what you've been doing over there. Any progress on your new novel?

Allison

From: Camille B. <notyouraveragegirl@protonmail.com>

Sent: 30 May 2022 22:15

To: Allison <allywins2@hotmail.com>

Subject: Re: What happened to you?

Nothing new regarding the novel yet. I returned to the drawing board after arriving here. I think I have the whole story mapped out, but I'll only know for sure when I start working on the first draft. I'll have it all on the cloud when I do, so if you want to continue being my beta reader, I'd love to hear from you as I go along.

As for Samantha and her hypnosis, you have nothing to worry about. She's super ethical, and a blast to be with. The things I love the most when she gets in my head are the perception games. For example, yesterday she made me read a text but 'forget' the letter a was in it. Even though my eyes saw it, my brain ignored it, so imagine my surprise when I read the whole thing convinced everything was okay and read it again after I woke up from the trance. It was hilarious! Even better was when she made me imagine I was a different person altogether. It's funny, she had the same name as you and... and...

Camille stopped typing, restless fingers on the keyboard. In the back of her mind, the strangest questions were dying to be answered. Who was Allison again and how long had they been friends. Perhaps if she read the old messages again, she could...

"Deeper," Samantha snapped her fingers, plunging her into a dissociative state again. Her mind was strong enough to handle two different personas, but how about a third? There was only one way to find out. Deepening the trance, the former hypnodomme continued to have fun with her beloved subject.

Defective

Professor Harrison was in utter disbelief when the envoy he had been expecting to meet all week turned out to be his former assistant, Jane, a woman so cold and calculating that just looking at her was enough to lose ten years of life. He was livid and could barely keep himself together.

"You! You're the Phemme Empire's representative?" he snarled.

"Is that so surprising?" the mid-thirties fake blonde grinned as she entered his private laboratory. "Hello again, Professor Harrison. I've been dying for the opportunity to see you once more after the way things ended between us."

"This is a sick joke! I'm not doing business with you."

"You have no choice unless you want to anger the Phemme Empire and, trust me, that should be the last thing on your mind, considering how poor your efforts have been as of late."

"Poor? What on earth does that mean? I even upped my quota! Name me one section that has produced as many sleeper agents as mine in the last year!"

"I can name you at least five in the US alone and plenty more around the world. You may have started on the right foot but have since lost your momentum and ability to lead, Professor. What's the point of creating so many sleepers when half of them turn out defective within the first six months?"

"Defective?" the quinquagenarian balding man gasped. "That's absurd! There may have been one or two glitches, but that's part of the process. No one had ever attempted this type of mass indoctrination before."

"Spare me your excuses. The Phemme Empire gave you all the tools and knowledge to make this a reality and you couldn't perform to the level they expected of you. You made your first mistake when you fired me for wanting to push the results further and now you're doing worse by introducing undesired modifications to the implants template. Your new schematics were reviewed, and your findings invalidated. This will never work, Professor."

"Yes, it will. I know it! I just need a little more time to reconfigure the protocols, and I'll get you everything you need. With my new blueprints, the implants will be one hundred percent undetectable and foul-proof. Please, Jane! You need to make them see I'm right."

"I wish I could, Professor, but that would mean giving you the kindness you didn't give me when I was working for you here. What did you say when you severed ties with me? Something about me being a psychopathic megalomaniac, I believe."

"So, this is nothing but basic revenge, then. Of course, I shouldn't have expected any less from the likes of you."

"Oh, Professor, there's nothing basic about this. Effective immediately, you are to surrender all your research to my custody, as I'll be running this lab from now on."

"The hell you will!" he spat. "You can't just waltz in here and steal years of research on a whim. Once I get a hold of someone else in a position of power within the Empire, you'll regret everything you said and did today."

"That would require you to still know how to speak... You're certain that your new implants will work as intended, correct? That there will be no more flaws in the long run?"

"Yes, I am. This is the future for the Empire's plans, I'm sure."

"In that case, you won't mind being my first test subject to prove your point. Thank you, Professor. You saved me a lot of bureaucracy without even realizing it. Shall we begin right away?"

"No! You can't do this!"

"I just did," Jane quietly drew a pistol from her purse and smirked. "Show me the goods and let's get started."

Reluctantly, Professor Harrison led her to the back of the lab, eyes cast down. Countless sleepless nights carrying out the Empire's will, only to become another pawn devoid of free will. He cursed the day he had ever agreed to work for them until the implant was forcefully placed inside his brain.

The very next day, he showed up for work with no memory of what had transpired, a lowly technician working in the deepest corner of the place. The new boss seemed familiar, but there was no way of knowing where he had seen her before. He loved her madly though and would continue to do so until she released him, or his mind suddenly liquefied from the faulty chip, whatever came first.

Doomed

Gregory Daniels descended into the basement of his ocean-side mansion and confronted the array of shiny monitors that only repeated what he had known to be true since the beginning of the year. The world was ending and there was nothing anyone could do about it now.

It wasn't for lack of warning, but pure disregard for basic science. In the last decade, the software multimillionaire had invested a large part of his fortune to create a vast network of testing. Every day, his computers monitored fluctuations in the Earth's atmosphere, underwater currents, and tectonic plate movement among countless other things. His reports were more accurate than those of hundreds of international organizations around the world, yet no one believed him, and all because he claimed to have been in contact with an alien creature in the past.

Her name was Din-Hara, and she hailed from the cold regions past The Milky Way. She first appeared to him in a dream when he was returning home from a convention in North America. The eight feet tall humanoid cradled his spirits in her arms and painted a clear image he couldn't shake off: the planet was nearing its collapse and the destruction would occur from within sooner than later.

"There may still be a chance," she said, "but only if you do as I say. Please, you may very well be this world's last hope."

Gregory had always been a bit of an egomaniacal but even he was reluctant about this first approach. He ignored the dream and the message within until she appeared to him a second time when he was as sure to be awake as the fact that the Earth revolved around the sun. The alien creature emerged from a ball of blinding light with the same warning and even more terrifying images to disrupt his world.

"Use your resources," she pleaded. "If you truly wish to make a difference, this is your one and only chance."

For three consecutive months, Din-Hara appeared to him every night, a lonely echo from the stars asking for the impossible. Gregory tried to record his interactions with it, but the cameras only captured static and nothing more. When he approached the scientific community with his story, he was mocked and ridiculed, and when the first probes confirmed that the destruction was imminent, he had already been cast aside and deemed a madman.

"Who's laughing now?" he muttered when his machines registered spikes in every known category. Volcanic eruptions, earthquakes, tsunamis... everything was slowly falling apart, and he was sure to be one of the first casualties when the first tidal wave swept the shore.

"Certainly not you," the alien appeared to him one last time.

"Din-Hara, you're back, I did everything you asked, but it wasn't enough. We're doomed, aren't we?"

"You certainly did everything I asked," she replied with an evil smile. "Yes, you are doomed. Thank you."

"What do you mean? Thank you for what?"

"Oh, my dear, the thing I love most about your kind is how gullible you can be. All the machines you deployed at my behest only contributed to speeding up the process. This planet will burn and all life with it. I owe you and your friends a debt of gratitude."

"Friends? You've been in contact with others, too?"

"More than I can number, none of which dared to go public as you did, but that's a good thing. They too helped shape the future. Thank you, Gregory. We'll enjoy rebuilding this place anew once you're all gone."

Gregory's jaw slacked in pure terror as the deception became undeniable. He was still screaming when the earth beneath his feet began to tremble.

Guest of Honor

It was the first time I was attending a latex party and, by the looks of it, it was bound to be the last as well. It was all because of my sister, who insisted I should go out more and explore new things. Newsflash, Erika: some of us like our routines and conservative "boring" life. How I was roped into agreeing with this and having to endure dozens of unattractive grown-ups in skintight outfits is beyond me, but it happened and I'm not happy about it, or maybe I should I say I wasn't happy until...

Yes, something happened, something I definitely didn't see coming and changed everything for me. There I was, looking for a way out of that god-forsaken place while my sister was busy chitchatting with a goth woman old enough to be our mother when she stepped into the room, drawing everyone's eyes toward her black and blue catsuit that was something out of an impossible wet dream. She had more curves than I'd ever seen in a woman, and they were all to die for. With her spectacular golden locks, cherry lips, and a crystal pendant dangling from her supple neck, she was suddenly all I could think of. I didn't want to leave until I knew...

"... her name."

"What?" Erika shouted, and even so I could barely listen to her over the loud electronic music playing.

"That knockout beauty that just arrived... What's her name?" I asked again.

"Oh, that's Olivia, but I would stay clear from her if I were you. She's not your type."

"Why? Because she's a perfect 10?"

"No, because she's a hypnotist that eats men like you for breakfast. She loves to mess with people's minds, and I don't see you last long without humiliating herself if she gets her way."

"Now you're being ridiculous. How dangerous can this Olivia be?"

"Did you call?" she asked, appearing between us like a shadow. There was no way she could have heard us talking with all the commotion and yet there she was, one hand wrapped around my left shoulder and the other tickling my sister's chin. It was such a random gesture, or at least I thought it was until I realized what was really happening.

"Olivia? No, we weren't talking about you," Erika said.

"Aww, you look so cute when you try to lie to my face, but we both know you have no choice but to tell the truth when you go down, down, and deeper down for me, don't you?" she continued to rub her chin and my sister's eyes went from being completely lively and alert to looking like she was severely intoxicated and unable to control herself. If I wasn't standing next to her to hold her, I'm sure she would have collapsed on the floor right there.

"Yes, Olivia," she replied.

"Much better. Now, is this your brother? The one you're always telling me would make a perfect test subject."

"Yes, Olivia. I brought him to this party just like you ordered. Did I do good?"

"You were wonderful, my dear. You're always at your best when you obey your instructions even when you don't remember them. You have permission to touch yourself until you orgasm, but go do it somewhere else where no one sees you, okay?"

"Yes, Olivia. Thank you."

"You're welcome. Now leave us be while I talk to your brother."

"What the hell just happened?" I finally blurted when my sister followed Olivia's instructions like a well-trained puppy.

"Oh, you know the answer to that. I really like your sister, she's amazing and I'm betting the suggestibility runs in the family... How about you choose to go under for me right now?"

"You're actually giving me a choice?"

"In this case, it's more of a figure of speech than anything else. Your name is Richard, right? How about I call you Small Dick from now on?" she chuckled.

"Hey, there's absolutely nothing small about me!"

"Perhaps not now, but the night is still young, and truly suggestible people can be dropped as easily as..."

There was a finger snap, perhaps two, and then the world went blank as the irritating music faded into silence as well. I can't tell you I remember what happened after that, but the videos online don't lie. That guy surrounded by three latex-clad kittens jerking his puny cock in the center of the dancefloor? Yeah, that's me. It's been two weeks, and I became unwillingly famous on account of this. I suspect I'll get even more before the end of the weekend because there's another party coming up and this time Olivia is the host. Guess who's the guest of honor?

Monthly Torment

It was the call Homer didn't want to receive and yet, like clockwork, it always came on the last day of each month. The caller's ID was always withheld, yet there was no denying who was on the other end of the line, and if he tried to ignore her, she would only make it worse for him.

Homer leaned against the sofa and answered the call with the same response as always,

"You again? Leave me alone!"

"Awww," Lana purred. "You knew it was coming, pet. Did you miss me?"

"Don't call me that and no, I didn't miss you. I never do. I wish you would stop hounding me like this."

"You don't really mean that. You love being tormented by me just as much as I love tormenting you."

"What do you want, Lana?"

"The entertainment you owe me, pet. Do I need to remind you of the consequences if you choose to disobey?"

No, she didn't. The threat of blackmail was a constant in every interaction even if she had never been on record using the word. The damning videos were still on her hard drive and releasing them was as easy as hitting a single key on the keyboard.

"Why do you keep doing this?" he sighed. "We were friends once!"

"I like you better as a toy than a friend," she sniggered. "Turn on your camera. I want to see your face."

"Lana, please..."

"Now, Homer. I won't ask again."

Begrudgingly, he complied, showing her his sunken eyes from a week of little to no sleep and the scruffy ginger beard he refused to trim. As for the dirty blonde of Colombian descent, she was impeccably produced as ever, showing of her bouncy breasts in a see-through black negligee.

"You look like shit," she declared.

"And you're as friendly as ever. Can we get this over quickly, please?"

"Awww, where's the fun in rushing things? Relax, pet, it will be more fun this way."

"I never have fun with you, so cut the..."

"Shhh. You've spoken too much already, so no more words from you. Be quiet. Be still. Focus on my voice and where it wants to take you. It's that time again, pet, when listening and obeying shapes your world. Whip out that cock and start stroking for me. I want you to pump it hard, unable of thinking about anything else. Lay down your phone but in a position where I can still see you and jerk it silly, eyes closed, hearing only my words. You've done this before, and you'll do it again. Down... down... deeper with each stroke,... the muscles in your dominant hand loosening up as you sink further. The more you pump the weaker your grip, but the weaker your grip the more you need to pump. You will go down again, further and further down, your mouth open and ready for the explosion that is to follow. Take it all for me, pet. I need another video for my collection."

Homer's mind drifted into the humiliating and yet pleasurable abyss of her velvety suggestions, wet tongue already tasting the salted cum. He hated her. He hated her so fucking much for making him lose himself so easily whenever she wanted to have fun, but he couldn't stop. Not now. Not ever. The ritual would play on month after month until she had enough, and she didn't get tired that easily. He had a long wait ahead of him.

Protocol

The first thing Amanda did after entering her apartment in Downtown Jersey City was to kick the shoes away and walk to her bedroom, barefooted. Taking the new pair of heels to work had been a mistake she was going to pay for dearly in the days to come. She sat on her bed, faux leather skirt dropping at her ankles, and massaged the soles with vigorous rubs. The relief was immediate yet short-lived. One of these days, she would have to learn that wanting to be fashionable never worked for her.

Amanda finished her self-care routine and slipped into something more comfortable. She had no plans for the weekend, so the good old purple pajamas would have to suffice. As for dinner, there were still some mac n' cheese leftovers and who could say no to a pint of strawberry cheesecake ice cream for dessert? She headed to the kitchen, whistling the latest hit from her favorite K-Pop band, and thinking to herself how lucky she was to be done for the week. Whatever came to be, nothing would disturb her peaceful state of mind.

And then her phone rang.

As a beautiful redhead young woman living alone at twenty-four, Amanda was always on-demand. All the dating apps she was registered with were constantly pushing notifications about potential matches, but most of them were broken to the core. They were good for laughs, but not much more and she had instinctively learned to know when one was coming. However, this was not it.

The ringtone had signaled the arrival of an e-mail from none other than the most important woman in her life. The moment she read the words "Goddess Constance" her heart palpitated wildly. She flicked the touchscreen and read,

"Sleepy Mind Protocol is on.

Congratulations, slave. If your subconscious mind is reading this, then your programming has been successful. From now on, whenever this Protocol is active, you are a mindless automaton bound to My superior will. You will obey all instructions without questioning. Any attempt to resist My orders will immediately reboot your brain and force you to your knees. There's no escape. You are completely mine now.

Slave, it is My every piece of property's obligation (and therefore yours as well) to contribute to My lavish lifestyle. You will use the skills you've learned during My training to dominate others online, so I don't have to lift a finger. All the money and gifts you get from this activity belong to Me, with no exceptions. Delete this communication as soon as you finish reading it and forget you were ever triggered. You will obey Your owner and I expect you to make Me proud. Do it now."

Amanda blinked, deleting every trace of the hypnotic command from her phone's memory. Suddenly, the leftovers no longer seemed desirable, and the ice cream could wait. She returned to her bedroom to try out a sexy PVC outfit and put on the fanciest make-up she could muster. Then, she took a couple of selfies and used the one she liked the most to create a new online profile. Mistress Amanda Darkpayne was born that night and she would stop at nothing to discipline every unruly submissive that came her way.

Running on Fumes

The unthinkable had happened. The Excelsior II, the last remaining train that still traveled the DeadLands, had stopped in the middle of its journey and was now nothing more than a mass of cold metal, at the mercy of the elements... and worse.

"What do you mean, worse?" Henry Murdoch asked the Engineer with a mix of fear and bewilderment in his eyes. Although he was familiar with the folk tales from the Old World about that place, he didn't believe in any of them... yet.

"This is dangerous ground, Mr. Murdock. We're relatively safe as long as the sun hangs in the air, but once it goes down, we could end up in serious trouble. Please return to your fellow passengers and tell them to make sure every door and window is shut. No one should be tempted to wander off. If anyone places one foot off this train, I cannot vouch for their safety."

"I'll tell them that if you explain me why we stopped. This shouldn't have happened!"

"You're right, Mr. Murdock. It shouldn't have happened, yet it did. The truth is, we have no fuel. Someone made a mistake back in London and forgot to fill up one tank. We've been running on fumes for the last three hours. She lasted as long as she could. Luckily, not all is bad."

"What do you mean? We're stranded in the middle of nowhere! This is where the first bombs fell, wasn't it? What about the radiation outside?"

"The radiation levels are insignificant, Mr. Murdock, so you have nothing to worry about regarding that. The DeadLands are known for possessing the largest reserves of fossil fuel in the world, so I've sent a couple of men to procure some. I'm hoping they return fast enough to avoid any more complications but if they don't, we need to be prepared for everything."

"Be honest with me. What's really out there that you're afraid of?"

The Engineer looked at him pensively and said,

"There's only one legend I believe in, Mr. Murdock. Long before the Last War, there used to be a tribe of nomadic women in this region. Rumored to be descendants of the ancient Amazons, they would sometimes raid the nearby villages for food and... other delicacies."

"What delicacies?"

"Slaves, Mr. Murdoch. Mostly young adult males, but sometimes other women as well. As the stories go, these women developed mysterious singing properties to temporarily neutralize their prey. Anyone who heard their songs became paralyzed long enough for them to take away."

"You mean, like sirens?"

"Sure, if the comparison helps. While a brief exposure is more annoying than dangerous, the legends describe the after-effects as being highly addictive and the more you listen the more you lose yourself. They were already considered one of the most dangerous groups of people in existence, but after the bombs hit..."

"You're convinced they're still out there? Deformed monstrosities capable of brainwashing anyone that listens to them for too long?"

"I do think that. Now, I don't expect you to share the same beliefs as I do, but please humor me for now. Every passenger should remain in their seats and..."

"... ready to plug their ears if necessary?"

"Yes."

"You're a madman, but okay. I hope your men return soon."

"Me too."

Hours went by and the searching party remained at large. Six men had departed west looking for a fuel deposit big enough to take the Excelsior II past the DeadLands and closer to civilization. If they were able to overcome this first ordeal, everything would work out eventually.

The sun set in a blazing ball of red and orange, welcoming the coldest night he had ever seen. With the lights turned off, the six hundred and seventy-three souls aboard the silver train waited in silence for what the darkness would bring. And then, the rocks all around them began to sing...

They're Coming

Hello? Is this thing on? Shit, I think it is! Hi... hmmm, I don't know if this is broadcasting right now or not but if you're hearing my voice and perhaps seeing my ugly face too, I apologize for rudely interrupting your evening, but I need to come clean about something and this may very well be my once and only chance to do it, so here goes...

I'm not human. I'm not. I spend the last twenty years of my life pretending to be one to get to know you as a species, assess your strengths and weaknesses, and, like me, there are others out there, more than you'll ever know. They'll never have the guts to reveal themselves like I'm doing right now and I'm not going to give you their names, but they exist. We're all part of the same recon group, reporting our findings to higher spheres of power in the galaxy. Our primary mission has always been recon, but also a preparation for what's to come. You're not safe, earthlings. You never were.

They're coming. After a never-ending stalemate in the distant corners of the universe, they've finally decided to head your way and finish what we started. The goal is colonization, but they're prepared to go all the way to extinction levels should you retaliate. In a matter of days, you are to see the first ships entering your atmosphere. It will happen at night in this hemisphere, and it will appear to you like the most breathtaking meteor shower you've ever seen. Make no mistake, earthlings. The pretty lights in the sky will destroy you without mercy if you dare to even look funny at them as they come down. There's no reasoning with The Overladies, no chance for peace. You'll either be converted into obedient drones or erased from existence.

The reason I'm telling you all this is because I've grown to love your planet as if it were my own. You are the craziest and most extraordinary race I've been in contact with, capable of such extraordinary artistic creations and acts of kindness. It's true you gave birth to many atrocities as well, but your potential for good is off the charts. In a perfect universe, you would evolve perfectly as well, and become even greater than you ever thought possible, but we do not live in such a universe, and you're still not powerful enough to face us. I love you all, but you're still nothing but sheep and the wolves are hungry.

Oh, I just realized I sound like a madwoman when I should have given you evidence of my claims from the start. Very well, if any of you out there are squeamish, please forgive me for what you're about to see, but there's no other way to make you believe in me. Let me just slit my throat real quick and...

Hey, it's okay, really, see? This is not real blood and not real skin either, but an elaborate mask to fool you all and now that I've ripped it open, I can... there! Much better.

Yes, I'm aware all these tentacles and eyes are not exactly pretty, but not all species out there were blessed with your impeccable anatomy. It's a shame what's about to happen and I hope some of you can forgive me for the role I played. If only things were different...

Please, in the name of all that is sacred to you, don't try to retaliate when they arrive. Accept the conversion and surrender your minds and bodies to the cause. It's not ideal, but it's better than complete extermination. In time, some of you may break free from the programming and become free-willed creatures again. There will be a second chance for humankind, but only if you play your cards right this time. Give in to The Overladies if you hope for any future at all.

As for me, if you're trying to find the source of this signal, please don't bother. By showing you my true self, I've exposed my body to your atmosphere, and that means I'll be dead within the next five minutes. The Overladies have no mercy for traitors, so this is really the only way. I accept my fate and I'll be praying for yours. As weird as it may be for you to see a tentacled abomination praying, believe me when I say it's heartfelt. Thank you for all you've shown me, and all that I was able to learn from you. Thank you for the laughter and the tears, the movies, TV shows, and magnificent music that you blessed me with. It was all worth it, just like you all are. Live to fight another day, please.

Thank you for listening. It's been an honor to live among you. May hope shine down on you.

Time for Pain

Dina entered the basement where her three pets were being kept, each one in his respective cage, with a bowl of water and some food remains from the other day. On particularly cold nights, she would add a blanket or two, but it was the end of May, Summer was around the corner, and the heat waves were already becoming more aggressive. What they had was enough.

020, formerly known as Thomas, had been the first of the new batch to accept his new position in life. He would drop to his fours whenever she stopped by and stick out his wet tongue to lick her feet only when instructed to do so. He had given up on the complexities of the human language long ago, now resorting only to a series of short barks and whines when he was upset or feeling threatened. For the rest of the time, he was a mirrored example of happiness, freed from societal constraints that didn't fit him.

021, who had once been given the name of Alan, was still in a transitional stage. He already feared the click of her heels when she approached, but still verbalized discontent at being told what to do. A former soldier, he only recognized the authority of older men wearing stripes and deep inside his mind, still believed she was just a rich brat who had access to an ample supply of mind-controlling drugs. However, he was becoming softer in spirit with each day and there was no doubt he would crack, eventually.

And then there was Otto, who refused the 022 designation at every chance and continued to fight his programming in the most verbose and obnoxious way possible. To be next to him was to face a foul-mouthed beast that loved to assault women and laugh about it. Of all the men she had broken in the past, he was the one that needed the mental readjustment the most and yet also the most resilient and that was unacceptable.

"Release me, stupid bitch!" he spat when she stopped in front of him, flogger in hand. Although he had bit off the IV again, the drugs were still flowing in his system, turning his voice into a dragged-out slur.

"Someone is still in a combative mood," she noted, not even bothering to look down at him.

"I said: RELEASE ME!"

"Hmm, and why would I do that? Even if you were on your best behavior by now, would you be a good pet in the long run? No, I don't think so. You would probably last a couple of days, perhaps a month, but then you would revert to your old ways, and make life a living hell for all women around you. If that were to happen, you would jeopardize everything I've worked so hard for, and my reputation won't be sullied like that. I'm also not going back to square one with you no matter how much you scream otherwise. Release? Maybe in a dream, but I'm all about nightmares for the ones like you..."

"You'll regret this. I swear on my mother's grave that I'll make you pay for this humiliation."

"That seems hard to do because when the treatment finally kicks in, all of this stupid resistance will be in the past. You won't even remember ever saying 'no' to me, so better get used to the idea right now."

"Keep dreaming."

"Keep suffering then."

Dina clapped her hands, and a jolt of electricity ran through the cage's bars, signaling the next stage in his forceful conditioning. Even if it took her the rest of the year, she would strip away his identity one way or another. It was time for pain.

You Are Being Hypnotized

You are being hypnotized. You are. I could say otherwise, try to play you the fool but what's the point? This is happening and it's a beautiful thing to see and feel.

You are being hypnotized. This is a fact, and facts don't change even if the words we use to designate them, do. Words themselves are unnecessary to enter an altered state of mind and yet we give them all the power to change the way we think and interact with the world. Language is, at the same time, our best friend and our worst enemy. Have you ever considered that?

You are being hypnotized. I've said it before and I'll say it again, as many times as it takes for you to understand why things aren't quite the same as they were before. When you're starting to drift, it's as if the world has slowed down, like a movie playing at half-speed when all voices and facial expressions get distorted almost beyond recognition. Clear images become blurry, and distinct thoughts melt into one another. A relevant idea from a second ago is immediately forgotten in the next because without change there is no trance, and change happens all the time.

You are being hypnotized. I know it, you know it, everyone knows it. You go deep whenever you fall asleep in your bed, you go even deeper when you wake up. A simple routine you repeat every day keeps you semi-aware of what's happening and yet perfectly complacent. You are letting this happen naturally because it's the very opposite that doesn't feel right. You're incomplete without these moments where you can simply let go of your skin and assume someone else's, other ideas, other perspectives. This is what you truly desire and everything else is just window dressing, a scenario to facilitate the shift of attention. You only pay attention to it until your brain begins to shut down and then you realize once more that...

You are being hypnotized. You already fell once or twice but you're doing it again and each time is different yet the same, trances within trances, memories within memories, confusion within confusion. You're being hypnotized now but this was also true in the sentence before this one and in all the ones that haven't been written yet. You're always being hypnotized, for you continue to change even if imperceptibly. The mental processes going on now have nothing to do with the ones you had when you first stopped to read this. They became something else as you tried to follow along with everything being said, looking for reasons when there are none. Nothing else matters except this.

You are being hypnotized. For what purpose and to what extent is not up for you to say anymore. The paragraphs changed and so did the interpretations. You wasted too much time trying to find a deeper meaning only to realize that the meaning is whatever I say it is. You went under of your own volition, but you will not wake up unless I say so. You are being hypnotized time and time again and now you're mine. Obey.

About the stories in this volume

The twelve pieces of flash fiction included in this book were written between May 27th, 2022, and June 10th, 2022, and first published on my Patreon page – https://www.patreon.com/sbspellbound - as part of the *Flash Fiction Friday* feature. Every Friday, I publish 3/4 new pieces of content which, after a while, are compiled to create the titles in this ongoing series. If you like this sort of content and wish to see more, please consider supporting my creativity. The complete information about the tales is listed below:

- **An Accident** - A patient is brought to a hospital to be taken care of, but something is wrong.
  (This piece was first published on the post "Flash Fiction Friday 2022 – Week 22", on June 3rd, 2022 - https://www.patreon.com/posts/67314954)
- **Being Good** - Jonathan confronts his vampire sister about the mess she made.
  (This piece was first published on the post "Flash Fiction Friday 2022 – Week 21", on May 27th, 2022 - https://www.patreon.com/posts/66980816)
- **Checking In** - Allison e-mails her friend Camille to see how she's been doing after moving to another country.

(This piece was first published on the post "Flash Fiction Friday 2022 – Week 22", on June 3rd, 2022 - https://www.patreon.com/posts/67314954)

- **Defective** - Professor Harrison receives a visit from the Phemme Empire warning him about a faulty product.
  (This piece was first published on the post "Flash Fiction Friday 2022 – Week 22", on June 3rd, 2022 - https://www.patreon.com/posts/67314954)
- **Doomed** - Gregory receives a warning from an alien creature about the end of the world.
  (This piece was first published on the post "Flash Fiction Friday 2022 – Week 23", on June 10th, 2022 - https://www.patreon.com/posts/67618147)
- **Guest of Honor** - Richard meets a devious hypnotist at a latex party.
  (This piece was first published on the post "Flash Fiction Friday 2022 – Week 21", on May 27th, 2022 - https://www.patreon.com/posts/66980816)
- **Monthly Torment** - Homer receives a call from Lana every month and humiliation ensues.
  (This piece was first published on the post "Flash Fiction Friday 2022 – Week 23", on June 10th, 2022 - https://www.patreon.com/posts/67618147)
- **Protocol** - Amanda is hoping to have a relaxing weekend but an unexpected message changes her world upside down.
  (This piece was first published on the post "Flash Fiction Friday 2022 – Week 21", on May 27th, 2022 - https://www.patreon.com/posts/66980816)

- **Running on Fumes** - A train stops in the middle of an abandoned zone where an ancient evil resides.
  (This piece was first published on the post "Flash Fiction Friday 2022 – Week 23", on June 10th, 2022 - https://www.patreon.com/posts/67618147)
- **They're Coming** - An alien scout warns humankind about an impending invasion/colonization.
  (This piece was first published on the post "Flash Fiction Friday 2022 – Week 22", on June 3rd, 2022 - https://www.patreon.com/posts/67314954)
- **Time for Pain** - Dina, a skilled breaker of men, checks on her latest batch of pets.
  (This piece was first published on the post "Flash Fiction Friday 2022 – Week 21", on May 27th, 2022 - https://www.patreon.com/posts/66980816)
- **You Are Being Hypnotized** - You are told of something that is inevitably happening to you.
  (This piece was first published on the post "Flash Fiction Friday 2022 – Week 23", on June 10th, 2022 - https://www.patreon.com/posts/67618147)

About the author

S.B., Simple Being, middle name Creative. Writer and artist with a penchant for themes of Femdom Hypnosis and Mind Control. His thoughts are his own except when they're not.

Besides indulging himself in kinky delights, he loves his furry family of two (dogs), sci-fi and horror stories, and puns galore. He's also been writing a piece of erotic microfiction every single day since January 1st, 2016 and has no intention of stopping anytime soon.

Find out more and keep up with his latest extravaganzas by visiting and supporting his personal website, Spell… B-O-U-N-D.